Celebraciones / Celebrations

¡Feliz día de San Valentín!
Happy Valentine's Day!

Elizabeth Ritter

traducido por / translated by
Fatima Rateb

New York

Published in 2017 by The Rosen Publishing Group, Inc.
29 East 21st Street, New York, NY 10010

Copyright © 2017 by The Rosen Publishing Group, Inc.

All rights reserved. No part of this book may be reproduced in any form without permission in writing from the publisher, except by a reviewer.

First Edition

Translator: Fatima Rateb
Editorial Director, Spanish: Nathalie Beullens-Maoui
Editor, English: Melissa Raé Shofner
Book Design: Michael Flynn
Illustrator: Continuum Content Solutions

Cataloging-in-Publication Data

Names: Ritter, Elizabeth.
Title: Happy Valentine's Day! = ¡Feliz día de San Valentín! / Elizabeth Ritter.
Description: New York : PowerKids Press, 2017. | Series: Celebrations = Celebraciones | Includes index.
Identifiers: ISBN 9781499428421 (library bound)
Subjects: LCSH: Valentine's Day–Juvenile literature.
Classification: LCC GT4925.R57 2017 | DDC 394.2618–dc23

Manufactured in the United States of America

CPSIA Compliance Information: Batch #BW17PK: For Further Information contact Rosen Publishing, New York, New York at 1-800-237-9932

Contenido

Tarjetas para mi clase	4
Una fiesta en la escuela	12
La hora de la merienda	16
Una canción especial	20
Palabras que debes aprender	24
Índice	24

Contents

Cards for My Class	4
A Party at School	12
Snack Time	16
A Special Song	20
Words to Know	24
Index	24

Mañana es el Día de San Valentín.
Lo celebraremos en la escuela.

Tomorrow is Valentine's Day.
We will celebrate at school.

Mi papá me ayuda a hacer las tarjetas para mi clase.

My dad helps make cards for my class.

Utilizamos papel de colores, marcadores y pegamento.

We use colored paper, markers, and glue.

Hago una tarjeta especial para la señorita Jones.

I make a special card for Miss Jones.

Es morada y tiene muchos adornos brillantes.

It's purple and has lots of glitter.

Mi mamá hace pastelitos de fresa.

My mom bakes strawberry cupcakes.

Cuando llegamos a la escuela al día siguiente, nos encontramos con una sorpresa. ¡La señorita Jones había colgado corazones!

At school the next day, we get a surprise. Miss Jones hung up hearts!

Estamos ansiosos por repartir las tarjetas.

We can't wait to hand out our valentines.

Recibo ocho tarjetas de mis amigos.

I get eight cards from my friends.

Durante la merienda, comparto mis pastelitos. Emily le da a todo el mundo un trozo de chocolate.

At snack time, I share the cupcakes. Emily gives everyone a piece of chocolate.

Luego nos sentamos en círculo sobre la alfombra.

Then we sit in a circle on the rug.

Aprendemos una canción especial de San Valentín.

We even learn a special Valentine's Day song.

Todo el mundo aplaude y canta.

Everyone claps and sings.

Con todo nuestro amor:
¡Qué tengan un Feliz Día de San Valentín!

Sending lots of love your way.
Have a Happy Valentine's Day!

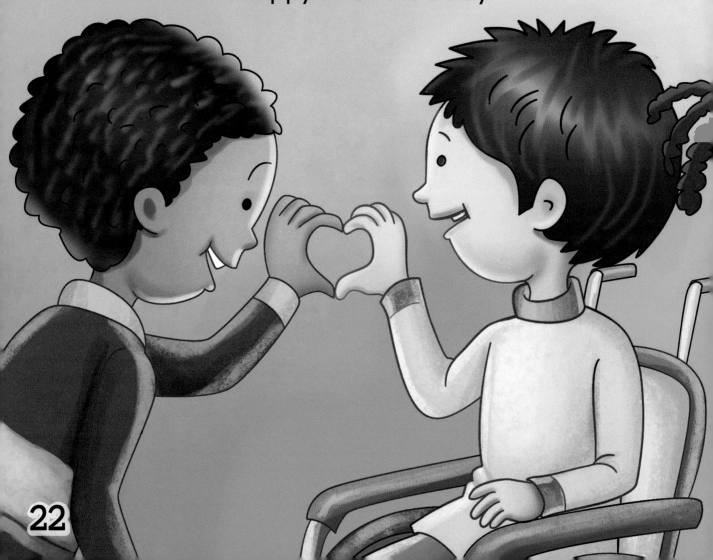

Palabras que debes aprender
Words to Know

(los) pastelitos
cupcakes

(el) pegamento
glue

Índice / Index

C
chocolate/chocolate, 17
corazones/hearts, 13

E
escuela/school, 5, 13

T
tarjeta(s)/card(s), 6, 8, 15